The Seven Silly Eaters

Written by MARY ANN HOBERMAN   Illustrated by MARLA FRAZEE

Voyager Books

Harcourt, Inc.

ORLANDO   AUSTIN   NEW YORK

SAN DIEGO   TORONTO   LONDON

For Debbie, Jane, and Richard
"When they were very young"
M.A.H.

In celebration of my Sito, Fudgie Kallel,
and the love so freely given through her daily work
M.F.

www.HarcourtBooks.com

First Voyager Books edition 2000
Voyager Books is a registered trademark of Harcourt, Inc.

The Library of Congress has cataloged the hardcover edition as follows:
Hoberman, Mary Ann.
The seven silly eaters/Mary Ann Hoberman; illustrated by Marla Frazee.
p. cm.
Summary: Seven fussy eaters find a way to surprise their mother.
[1. Food habits—Fiction. 2. Brothers and sisters—Fiction.
3. Stories in rhyme.] I. Frazee, Marla, ill. II. Title.
PZ8.3.H66Se   1997
[E]—dc20   95-18186
ISBN 0-15-200096-8

ISBN 0-15-202440-9 pb

O Q R P

The illustrations in this book were done in Pelikan transparent
drawing inks on Strathmore paper, hot press finish.
The display type was set in Blackfriar.
The text type was set in Weiss.
Color seperations by Bright Arts, Ltd., Singapore
Printed and bound by Tien Wah Press, Singapore
Production supervision by Pascha Gerlinger
Designed by Kaelin Chappell and Marla Frazee

Not so long ago, they say,
A mother lived—just like today.
Mrs. Peters was her name;
Her little boy was named the same.
Now Peter was a perfect son
In every way—except for one.

When Peter was just one year old,
He did not like his milk served cold.
He did not like his milk served hot.
He liked it warm . . .

                                    And he would not

Drink it if he was not sure
It was the proper temperature.

But Mrs. Peters did not mind.
She was a mother sweet and kind;
And when his milk spilled on the floor,
She patiently prepared some more.
She'd take the bottle from the shelf
And chuckle softly to herself,
"What a silly sort of eater
Is my darling baby Peter."

When Peter had not yet turned two,
Another baby sweet and new
Was born—dear Lucy, small and fair,
With big blue eyes and curly hair.
But long before this child was grown,
She had opinions of her own
Of what she'd eat and what she'd not.
She hated milk, both cold and hot,
And warm was worst of all. Instead
Whenever Lucy dear was fed,
She bellowed for pink lemonade,
Not from a can . . .

                              Oh, no . . .

Homemade.

But Mrs. Peters did not mind.
She squeezed each lemon to its rind
While mopping milk up from the floor
And patiently preparing more.
She'd take the lemons from the shelf
And giggle softly to herself,

"What a silly pair of eaters
    Are Lucy dear and Peter Peters."

Now Lucy grew and Peter grew
Till he was three and she was two.
And who was one? Why, little Jack
With eyes so brown and hair so black—
A happy baby, never cross,
But all *he'd* eat was applesauce.

Peeling apples by the pound,
Mrs. Peters faintly frowned.
She'd take the apples from the shelf
And murmur weakly to herself,
"What a silly bunch of eaters
Are Lucy, Jack, and Peter Peters."

Peter, Lucy, and young Jack
Had another brother, Mac.
Mac was charming, round and plump;
But if his oatmeal had a lump,
Mac would dump it on the cat.
(Mrs. Peters hated that.)

But since she loved her children four,
She'd strain the oatmeal two times more.
She'd take it from the pantry shelf
And mumble sadly to herself,
"What a foolish group of eaters
Are all my precious little Peters."

Before another year was through,
Who came along? Why, Mary Lou!
She was a darling, sweet and bright,
And had a healthy appetite.
(That is, as long as she was fed
Soft and squishy homemade bread.)

Poor Mrs. Peters got no rest
But still she did her very best.
She'd take the flour from the shelf
And mutter feebly to herself,
"What a fussy bunch of eaters
Are all my lovely little Peters."

A year rolled by.
The children grew.
"They really are a splendid crew,"
Sighed Mrs. Peters, pinning pins
And diapering her brand-new twins:
Little sisters, quick and smart,
Impossible to tell apart;
But Flo liked poached eggs, Fran liked fried.
If she mixed them up, they cried.

Tired to the very bone,
Mrs. Peters groaned a groan.
She'd take the eggs down from the shelf
And whisper weakly to herself,
"What persnickety young eaters
Are all my seven little Peters."

Now time went by as time will do;
And as it passed, the children grew.
The problem was that as they grew,
Their appetites kept growing, too!
But not their choice of what to eat:
Each child continued to repeat
They wanted what they'd had before—

The trouble was
They wanted *more!*

Creamy oatmeal, pots of it!
Homemade bread and lots of it!
Peeling apples by the peck,
Mrs. Peters was a wreck.

She wiped her brow and heaved a sigh;
Another year was passing by.
In fact, she realized with sorrow,
Her birthday would arrive tomorrow!
Drearily she shook her head
And wearily went up to bed.

She thought the children had forgot
Her special day—but they had not!
At crack of dawn they all began
To carry out their secret plan:
Mrs. Peters would be fed
A birthday breakfast in her bed!
A breakfast made of all the foods
That kept them in such happy moods.

So while their weary mother slept,
Down the stairs the children crept;
And from the cupboards and the shelves
Happily they helped themselves.

Cheerfully they chopped and stirred,
Preparing what they each preferred.
But despite the pains they took,
Since nobody knew how to cook,
To measure things or make them hot—
The more they tried, the worse it got!

First Mac's oatmeal turned out lumpy

Which made poor Mac turn grim and grumpy.

In fact, the lumps got him so cross,

He dumped them in Jack's applesauce.

This bothered Jack so much he threw

It in the dough of Mary Lou

Who tossed the mishmash that *that* made

Straight into Lucy's lemonade;

And that put *her* in such a huff
She poured the icky sticky stuff
Into the double frying pan
That held the eggs of Flo and Fran
Who flung the hodgepodge on the spot
Into the milk in Peter's pot!

But when they saw what they had done,
They wished they never had begun.
They'd hardly slept a wink that night
And still things hadn't turned out right.
And even though they'd tried their best,
It hadn't worked.
They were depressed.

They'd be in trouble, too, unless
They found someplace to hide the mess.
The oven seemed the perfect spot.
(They all forgot it still was hot.)
They stuck the pot inside and then
They all went back to bed again.

The clock struck six but on they slept.
Meanwhile their mother softly stepped
Down to the kitchen, smelled a smell.
What could it be? She could not tell.
It smelled so good. She sniffed some more
And opened up the oven door.

She woke the children with her cries.
They all came running in surprise,
And in the kitchen what they found
Was Mrs. Peters dancing round!
And in the oven, no mistake,
A pink and plump and perfect cake!

And as their mother danced with glee,
She cried, "A birthday cake for me?
A birthday cake still piping hot?
To think I thought that you forgot!
Now tell me please, how did you make
This pink and plump and perfect cake,
So high and light and smooth as silk?"

"It's smooth as silk from all my milk,"
Said Peter. Lucy said, "It's pink
From all my lemonade, I think."
"And from my apples," added Jack.
"My oatmeal made it soft," said Mac.
"My bread dough, too," said Mary Lou.
Said Fran and Flo, "As for its size,
It was our eggs that made it rise."
Then everybody sniffed some more,
And danced around the kitchen floor!

They put the cake upon a dish
And lit the candles. "Make a wish,"
The children cried, "before you blow!"
And Mrs. Peters did just so.
And what is more, her wish came true,
As birthday wishes always do.

And from that day to this, 'tis said,
The Peters family all is fed
A single simple meal—just one—
A meal that's good for everyone,
A meal on which they all agree,
Made from their secret recipe.

They all take turns in mixing it.
They all take turns in fixing it.
It's thick to beat and quick to bake—
It's fine to eat and fun to make—

It's Mrs. Peters' birthday cake!